Jazzy Joy,
Our Miracle Dog

Written

by

Caroline Joy Quinn

Illustrated

by

Sarah Hunter

October 2021

This book is dedicated to my miracles.

Tom,

Daniel,

David,

and

Jazzy Joy.

Before the Story Begins

This is the true story about a family that lost their beloved dog and the events that unfolded after his passing. Some of the names have been changed. No extra characters were added. It is not the most exciting story. There are no evil villains that superheroes must destroy. There are no fairy godmothers who cast magical spells making everything wonderful. Instead, it is a story from the heart that is being shared to encourage all to never give up and to keep looking for the good.

To best understand the main characters, it is important to know that Caroline and Tom believe in God. They were both strong believers in the power of prayer, and they have found peace in knowing that they are not alone. Over the years, Tom and Caroline have prayed over many issues and their faith has given them hope during the storms in their lives. In good times and in bad, they have continued to believe that God is over all. Caroline and Tom also believe that the creator of all, the God who hung the stars in the sky, is interested in their personal lives.

The author's hope is that this story will breathe hope into her readers and encourage them to deal with whatever losses and disappointments may come into their lives, whatever they may be. Sadly, loss is part of life and affects everyone very differently. Sometimes, but sadly not always, there are unexpected surprises and joys that come from loss. Sometimes, something wonderful comes out of something sad and broken. Life is hard at times, but God is ever faithful. Even in the darkest times, a glimmer of hope can help heal and mend broken hearts.

To fully understand the story, here is some background information. After leaving England more than twenty-five years ago, Caroline and Tom settled into life in Seattle. They were blessed with two amazing boys, and as a family they have enjoyed hiking and traveling together both here and abroad.

TOM

CAROLINE

DAN

DAVID

... AND SNUGGLES!

Chapter 1: Meet the Quinns

Dr. Tom Quinn is a well-known professor of astronomy and has taught astrophysics at the University of Washington for more than twenty-five years. In his spare time, this mountain man loves to explore hiking trails and enjoy the beauty of God's creation. His bushy beard suits him well, and even his students say it is necessary and appreciated. When he laughs his eyes twinkle, he smiles easily, and he is quite easy going. Years ago, Caroline fell deeply in love with her quiet and gentle man and they continue to love life traveling and growing together.

Caroline is a cheerful, tall, brown-haired gal, who is energetic, chatty, and creative. Happiest walking her dog and talking with friends, Caroline is passionate about living life to the fullest. Seeking beauty in all areas of her life, she can often be found organizing, gardening, arranging flowers, or playing on her grand piano. She loves to laugh, support garage sales, drink lattes, read, cook for her family, celebrate, and do something new every day. Teaching piano is her calling, and she finds great joy in finding the perfect music and writing arrangements for her delightful students. She has also volunteered for various causes over the years in their church and community.

Dan, their oldest son, is smart and is super busy working and building a career in music. Like mother, like son, and their love for music is a precious common bond that they share. Dan plays in a band and plans to become a music sound engineer. In his spare time he skis, bikes, hikes, and spends time with his friends.

David, their youngest, has a career in the military and has traveled the world serving his country. He is also very busy, focusing on fitness, nutrition, building a business, and pursuing a military career. Both boys are tall, strong, and love to play basketball and work out together.

And last, but not least, there is Snuggles. Their darling spaniel arrived just a few days before Christmas many years ago when the boys were very young. Snugs captured everyone's heart the night he arrived, and had been a precious family member ever since. All of Caroline's piano students adored Snugs, and were so excited to see him each week. Caroline quickly realized that her darling pet was the main attraction. Snugs even had his own song that Caroline composed, and her students loved it.

At the time of writing this story, David, the youngest son, is serving in the army. Dan, the eldest, is working and active in his music community and enjoys playing in his band, *The Boards*. Reflecting back over the years, in good times and during some tough times too, one thing had never changed: Snuggles had always been the glue that held the family together.

Chapter 2: A Peaceful Passing

So it was the worst day ever as the Quinn family watched their sweet Snuggles lying on the steel surgery table at the Northeast Veterinary Hospital. After battling a long illness, and having every test and treatment possible, the vet counseled the family, advising them to let Snugs go. There was nothing more that could be done. Knowing that the doctor was right, Caroline requested some time to gather her little family together. In record time, Tom arrived on his bike from the University, Caroline picked up Dan, and now they were standing around Snuggles.

As Caroline stroked his frail little body, and kissed him on top of his soft curly head, Snuggles seemed to know what was happening and did not struggle. Looking up at his dear family one last time, he seemed to be at peace. In his sweet, non-verbal way, he assured his loved ones that everything was going to be all right, and that there was no need to worry. It was time for the family to say their final goodbyes.

The grieving family watched the vet insert the needle into Snugs, and he closed his soft brown eyes for the last time. After a moment, Tom announced that his little heart had stopped beating. Completely devastated, the family huddled together and cried their hearts out. No words, only buckets of tears. Sweet Snugs had brightened their lives for more than fifteen years, and now he was gone. Snugs was no longer in pain, but his family's pain was just beginning.

Walking as if in a daze, like robots, they mumbled their thanks to the vet, paid the bill, and Tom hurried back to work. Back in the van, Dan and Caroline stared into space. Although Dan did his best to comfort his mom, the pain in her heart was too raw. After some time they decided to call David. Currently, David was in Texas serving in the army, and they knew that he would want to know. Snugs adored David, and they had shared a special friendship for many years. Although David was not totally surprised, since he knew that Snugs was dealing with some health issues, he was devastated. He had not been able to say goodbye to his long-time, four-footed little buddy. After some time, Caroline started the van and left the animal hospital parking lot. Knowing she needed to appear to be strong so Dan would not worry too much, she pasted on a smile, and drove Dan back to his place.

But as Caroline walked up the steps to the front door, she immediately missed seeing Snugs waiting by the window to welcome his family home. *How could everything have changed in such a short time?* Wandering around the house, there were reminders of Snugs everywhere. His blanket, and the blue plastic gloves and soiled towels that had been used to help treat his infection, were just as she had left them. Picking up everything as quickly as possible, Caroline threw everything out. *Coping would be less painful if everything was gone,* she thought. But when she saw the empty food bowl in the kitchen, she totally fell apart, crying until there were no more tears left inside. Snuggles wasn't coming back. Never again would Snugs jump up on the couch for a snuggle.

Chapter 3: Hurting Hearts at Thanksgiving

Snuggles died early in October, and everything changed. Caroline's little fluffy shadow that had followed her everywhere was now only a memory. Hikes were not as fun without the curly bundle of joy boldly charging up the mountains. Halloween came and went. This year there was no dog to dress up to amuse her students and trick-or-treaters. Nothing was fun anymore. Thanksgiving arrived, and although there were many reasons to be grateful, there was a silent heaviness in the air. Dealing with loss, whatever it may be, seems to be even more painful around the holidays. What should have been a joyous celebration was framed with grief. They missed Snugs more than they had ever imagined possible. Snugs had been a central part of every gathering, the life of the party, for so many years. Turkey and yummy pumpkin pie had been his favorites at Thanksgiving and Christmas.

To make matters worse, David, the youngest son, was also missing, unable to get leave to come home. It was a small gathering with only Dan, Tom, Caroline, and Tom's mother sitting at a very big table. Now serving in Germany, David was not able to get a holiday pass for Thanksgiving. Due to staffing needs at the army base, they would have to wait until Christmas to see David again. An empty chair, no Snuggles, and a broken heart. Beautiful food with all the fixings and hurting hearts. *Was this their new normal?* Caroline was smiling on the outside, but crying on the inside. And it was exhausting.

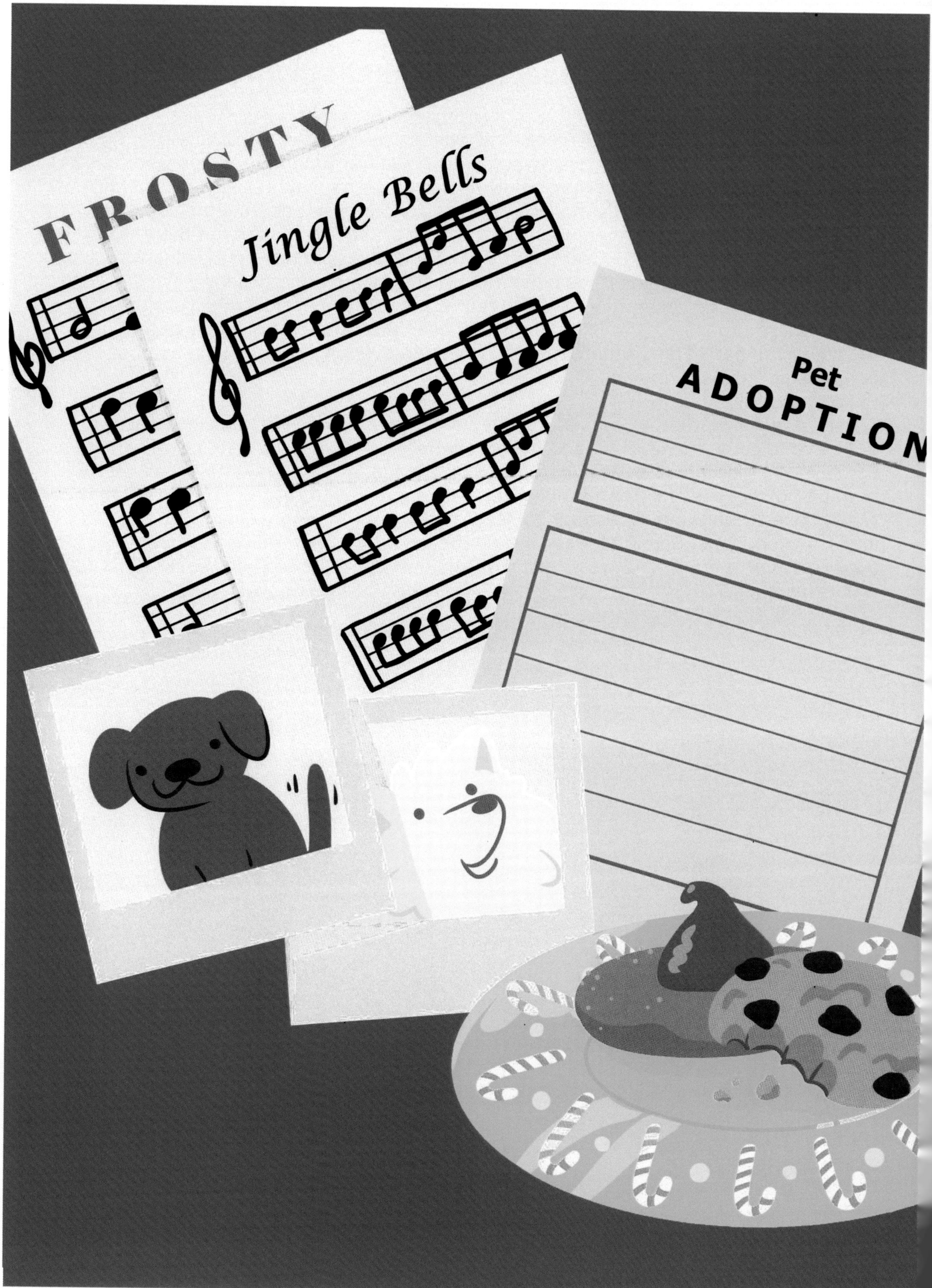
FROSTY
Jingle Bells
Pet
ADOPTION

Chapter 4: Closed Doors

Caroline continued to take one day at a time, teaching and focusing on her piano students and doing her best to be cheerful. Teaching the popular holiday tunes and carols was always fun, and the music was especially comforting. The holiday piano recital had gone very well, and now the students were getting excited about the upcoming Christmas break. Although attending parties and entertaining created a loose rhythm in the dreary, rainy month of December, everything seemed to take more of an effort. A family without a dog just didn't seem right, especially at Christmas. Anyone who has had a dog knows that they are like part of the family. And when they leave, they leave a huge hole in their family's hearts. *Perhaps it was time to think about getting a new dog,* Caroline thought. Snugs would not have wanted Caroline to be alone.

And so in early December, two months after Snuggles' passing, a new search began. Adoption seemed like a sensible idea. Many dogs needed good homes, and it seemed to make sense to move in this direction. Recently, Caroline's friends had adopted a dog from the local animal shelter, and it had been—and continued to be—a perfect fit. Still, it was a little scary. Since they had found Snuggles through a friend who was a breeder, adoption was going to be a new adventure. Hopefully it would be a good move.

But despite checking and rechecking many dog-adoption websites and talking to many animal shelters every day for more than a week, Caroline didn't have any success. This door seemed to be closed. It was surprising to discover that adopting a dog was not as easy as one would have thought it would be. Applications that were submitted were turned down due to various reasons. At one point, it looked like Caroline's application was going to be accepted. Sadly, the dog that was available needed lots of attention due to some particular special needs. Although Caroline's application was being considered as a good choice, in the end, the agency decided that a busy piano teacher would not be the best choice. Although the call from the agency was apologetic and reassuring, this door, at least for the time being, was closed. It was very discouraging.

Clearly, the adoption journey was going to take some time. Every morning, Caroline and Tom prayed for the right dog to join their family. Over the years, they had seen some amazing answers to prayer. Years ago, while still living in England, they had prayed for a job to open up for Tom. After waiting for months and receiving some rejections, God provided a job in Seattle. Leaving their dear friends in Oxford was very hard. Starting their new lives in Seattle, they had prayed for good friends and a good church where they could raise their family. So many doors had opened. God had brought just the right people into their lives at just the right time. Life-long friends. Forever friends. Over the years, they had prayed their hearts out for their boys asking for God's blessing and protection in their lives. But they had never prayed for a dog before. *Would God bring a dog into their lives in time for Christmas?* It was almost too much to hope for. But they kept praying and asking God for a dog that would love Caroline's students, love her friends, and would arrive in time for Christmas. Timing was everything. And time was running out.

Chapter 5: Running out of Time

Hoping to get into the Christmas spirit, Caroline and Tom bought their tree earlier than usual and decorated it together. It was harder this year. Adorable dog ornaments stayed in their boxes, and the fireplace seemed lonely with only three stockings hanging instead of five. Snuggles was no longer lying at her feet as she taught her students and no longer cuddled up by her side at night. Weeks after his passing, there were still lingering memories in every room. Caroline missed hearing Snug's clicky paws on the floor as he followed her all over the house. Even the students missed Snugs.

Then there was more bad news. After weeks of waiting, they learned David was not able to get leave to come home for Christmas. Another great loss. He had been deeply missed at Thanksgiving, and now they had to accept that David was not coming home for Christmas. Not fair … it's just not fair!! Although disappointed in the news, Caroline did her best to create a cozy, festive home, lighting lots of candles, wrapping gifts, sending out cards, baking Christmas goodies, and more, trying to feel content. Now two members of her family were missing.

Bittersweet. It was the perfect word to describe the early, gloomy days of December. Although they had been blessed in so many ways and were truly grateful, there always seemed to be a sadness lurking just below the surface. Friends had recently brought their newly adopted dog for a visit, and Caroline was thrilled to see them so in love with their new puppy. She knew so well the joy of watching a fluffy puppy with a wagging tail dance around, delighting all. But behind the smiles and compliments, her heart was hurting. Her teaching schedule kept her going, and she was grateful for full days. Focusing on her students, eating too much (not good), and waiting for her phone to ring with a call about a dog to adopt was the new daily routine. Christmas was such a crazy and busy time for everyone. What were the chances that a dog would come into their lives? Maybe she should just postpone the dog search until the New Year. Time slipped by. Christmas was only two weeks away.

Chapter 6: A Brilliant Option

Since she was running into dead ends exploring dog-adoption websites, Caroline decided to let her neighbors know that she was looking for a dog by posting on the neighborhood website Nextdoor. Maybe someone would know of someone with a puppy up for adoption. She was determined to check out every possibility and explore every path available.

And then, out of the blue, there was finally a breakthrough. WhoooooHOOOOO!! While checking her email one morning, Caroline was delighted to find a note responding to her post. After reading that Caroline was not having any success in adopting a dog, Mary, a sweet neighbor, reached out and suggested that Caroline consider becoming a foster mom. It turned out that Mary had a friend who ran a local dog-rescue agency called Little Blessings. *What a brilliant idea!* Moving on to plan B, Caroline decided to postpone trying to adopt a puppy until after the holidays. Instead, she would contact Little Blessings and see if there was a dog that needed a temporary home.

This was a new development, and the whole process certainly was taking some unexpected twists and turns. What would it like to be a foster mom for a dog? It was time to find out. Minutes later, Caroline was talking with the owner of Little Blessings, and a home visit was scheduled for the next day. Although not familiar with the rescue agency Little Blessings, Caroline learned that it was a respected local charity dedicated to placing stray dogs into foster homes for short periods of time. This provided the agency some time to look for prospective adoptive parents. Little Blessings provided those who were interested in adopting a dog an opportunity to spend time with the dogs.

Having prospective adoption parents spend time with the dogs in their homes gave future families an opportunity to be sure that the dog would be a good fit for their particular situation before making the final decision. Rushing into an adoption could be disastrous. Completing all of the required paperwork and checking the references needed for a successful adoption can take some time. Meanwhile, organizations such as Little Blessings provided the dogs with a safe place to stay during this process. Being a foster mom was a great way to assist the dog-adoption agencies, too, as they worked to find forever homes for stray dogs. And it was only a short-term commitment.

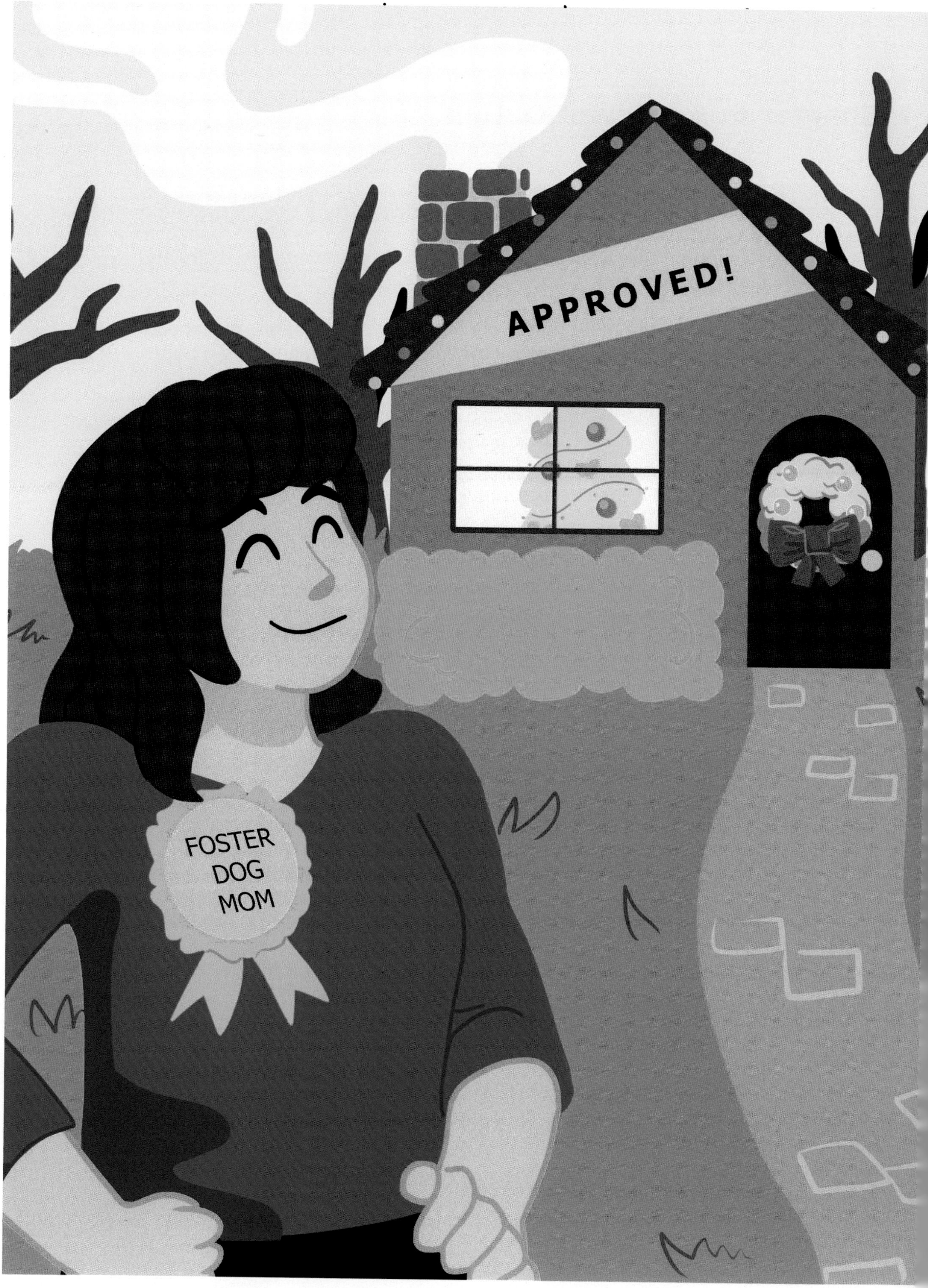
APPROVED!
FOSTER DOG MOM

Chapter 7: Little Blessings

When Nancy Smith, the owner of Little Blessings, came over for the in-home visit, it was clear immediately that she was extremely committed to finding suitable owners for the dogs. An hour later, after a thorough house check and a long interview, Caroline was delighted to be approved as a foster mom for dogs. It was quite a surprising turn of events. Although it was unlikely that Caroline would have her own dog in time for Christmas, it was possible that there could be a dog that needed a foster home for a short time. This seemed like a sensible plan. After promising to be in touch if there was a need, Nancy left, leaving Caroline alone with her thoughts.

Despite many unknowns, it was clear that the adoption door, at least for now, was closed. Caroline would try again in the New Year. As a person of faith, Caroline believed that when God closes a door, He opens a window. She had seen it happen many times in the most unexpected ways. Right now, it seemed that the open window was the opportunity to be a dog foster mom. Would they have a puppy in time for Christmas? What breed would he or she be? How long would the foster puppy need a home? Questions … and more waiting.

Little Blessings

There is a stray dog in California.
Are you interested?

YES!!!!

Chapter 8: Waiting

The long winter days dragged on. With her cell phone by her side and fully charged, Caroline constantly checked for new messages. Students came and went, and still there were no messages. Waiting was extremely stressful. With less than two weeks before Christmas, the days were ticking by. And then it happened.

Ping!! Hurray! It was a text message from Nancy. *Great news! A stray dog had been rescued in California and needs a foster home as soon as possible.* Caroline was asked if she would be interested. She responded immediately. *Yes!!* Seconds later, another new message popped up. The most adorable photo of a light brown cocker spaniel appeared on Caroline's screen. Her name was Winnie. What a sweetie! She seemed to be smiling. Caroline smiled back. Being a foster mom was going to be fun, even if it was only going to be for a short time.

Although they had hoped for a larger dog, they were looking forward to having Winnie for a short stay. She looked very small in the photo, and Caroline and Tom wondered how she would manage going on hikes. Snugs had been a larger dog, and this new dog seemed more like a puppy in the photo. Oh well, it was just for a short time. If she was too small, they would carry her in a backpack. They would figure something out. And most importantly, Winnie would be spared from being dropped off and left alone at an animal shelter.

Chapter 9: A Call from Nancy

Caroline learned that Winnie had been found wandering along a busy road high up in the rugged San Bernardino Mountains in California. The stray dog was now safe at Rosie's Home for Dogs, but sadly would not be able to stay there for long due to a lack of room. Someone who had recognized Winnie rescued the frightened puppy and took Winnie to Rosie's Home for Dogs. This kind soul had been the housekeeper to Winnie's owners and told Rosie that her owners had recently passed away. Due to full households and busy lives, the other family members were not able to give her a home. How tragic. Winnie was now homeless. What an urgent situation. A home was needed right away.

If a foster mom was found, Winnie would be safe. It was a horrifying fact that strays going to animal shelters in California generally did not have happy endings. Something must be done—and soon. But what? Caroline wanted to help the dog, but they lived a thousand miles away. How could they get Winnie to Seattle? By train? By plane? Would Rosie, the lady who ran the rescue home, be able to help? Her mind was racing with questions. And then there was another breakthrough.

It turned out that Rosie, who ran the rescue home for dogs in California, actually knew the owner of Little Blessings in Seattle. Believe it or not, Nancy and Rosie had met in college years ago. As friends, they had shared the same passion for caring for stray animals and had worked together at an animal shelter in California many years ago. Rosie had remained in California while Nancy settled in Seattle. It was actually Rosie who called Nancy about Winnie. What an incredible connection! No words, just wow!! With everyone working together, Winnie would be saved. A miracle was unfolding.

Due to Nancy's years of experience, she knew exactly what to do. If everything worked out according to plan, Winnie would be a passenger on the next available truck to Seattle. So many pieces needed to fall into place. And there were no guarantees. Caroline was determined to hold everything lightly. After all, even the best plans can change and come to an end. Holding everything lightly could avoid a massive disappointment.

Chapter 10: Getting Ready!

Since Caroline had given everything away after Snuggle's passing, it was time to go shopping. What great fun. Soon her shopping cart was full with dog food, a new bowl, a collar, a leash, dog treats, bones, and a soft, warm blanket for their soon-to-be new addition. And of course, toys. A dog can never have enough toys!! Everything was set except for one final touch. After putting the new supplies in the cupboard, Caroline once again opened her ornament box and selected all the spaniel ornaments that she had collected over the years. After placing each one lovingly on their tree, she hung their Christmas dog stocking with the others on the fireplace mantle. There was room for hope. But waiting was so hard. Although it was exciting time, it was also a time of anxiety with so many unknowns.

Would the new dog would be friendly? Shy? Afraid of strangers? Only time would tell. Given all that Winnie had been through, it was highly likely that she would be very scared and nervous. They would have to earn her trust, which would take time. Winnie would need time to adjust to her new surroundings. For Winnie, everything and everyone would seem strange and scary. She would need lots of space and patience in the early days. Reflecting on their early days with Snuggles, Caroline remembered that Snugs had loved their family right from the start and there had been no need for an adjustment time. Rain or shine, Snugs had been the best companion ever. Caroline was really looking forward to having a walking buddy again. She understood that Winnie would likely not have a personality like Snugs, but maybe things would work out. After all, it was only for a short time.

Chapter 11: Introducing Winnie

Ping! Another message from Nancy. More good news! Winnie would be arriving in five days. All of the arrangements had been made. There was no backing out now. Caroline and Tom were going to be dog foster parents for Winnie in five days. With a lighter heart, Caroline totally enjoyed her final teaching week before the break. Christmas music had never sounded better. The following days seemed a little easier and brighter and she was starting to get into the Christmas spirit.

Five days later, Tom and Caroline drove to the designated pickup spot in the middle of a fierce thunderstorm. At times, the visibility was so poor that it was quite worrying. At last, they arrived and parked their car. The designated pick-up site was at a gas station about twenty-five miles south of Seattle in Federal Way. More waiting. Precious cargo was on its way. Others were also waiting in their cars, while more continued to arrive. Caroline and Tom didn't know what to expect, but they knew that the fostering process would likely have some wrinkles.

Nothing was ever perfect and nothing was ever wasted. Years ago, a dear friend had shared a life-changing truth with Tom and Caroline. He wisely advised them not to let perfect be the enemy of the good. This fostering process may not be perfect, but they believed that it would be good. On a personal note, over the years, Caroline had learned that allowing herself to accept what is good rather than constantly seeking perfection, had freed her from a lifelong fear of failure. Being able to believe that her ideas were good had given her the confidence to start to write this story, to publish her piano arrangements, and to have the courage to jump in and take on new projects. In 2018, when they boarded the plane to begin Tom's year-long sabbatical in Canada, Australia, and Santa Barbara, Caroline did so knowing that good was waiting for them.

Now she was hoping for good again. It was a dark and stormy Sunday night, and they were grateful to have arrived safely. As sheets of rain pelted down outside, they waited warm inside their van. Both Caroline and Tom were beginning to wonder what they had gotten themselves into. And they were both secretly hoping that they were not making a big mistake.

For this fostering adventure to work out, Winnie would need to feel very safe and comfortable in their home. How long would it take for her to feel at home? And then there was the issue of Caroline's piano students. How would Winnie respond to her piano students? Snuggles had loved all her students and had particularly enjoyed all the tummy rubs from her adoring students. A barking dog would frighten her students. They had specifically prayed for a dog that would love her students and welcome them. Only time would tell.

At last, brilliant headlights came into view. After traveling more than one thousand miles, the truck pulled into the parking lot and came to a stop. Tom and Caroline giggled as they noticed the name painted on the side of the truck. The Wiggle

Butt Transport!! Such a cute name. Doors slammed and now many were gathering by the truck. In the pouring rain, prospective dog owners waited patiently.

Energetic volunteers jumped out, and in no time the side panel flew open. And then everyone marveled at the most incredible sight. Piled high in tidy rows were locked cages holding excited, barking dogs. They must be absolutely thrilled to breathe in fresh air after such a long stuffy ride. So many dogs … which one was Winnie? Bursting with anticipation, the eager couple stood in line waiting for their turn. One by one, names were called out, paperwork was signed, and the dogs were matched accordingly. Everyone seemed delighted with their new furry friends and Caroline watched them walk away as the line became shorter.

According to the paperwork that they had received from Nancy Smith, Winnie was nine years old, not a puppy anymore. As was previously mentioned, Winnie had been found while wandering along the highway in the San Bernardino Mountains in the beautiful state of California. This little gal had clearly suffered some huge losses. Winnie must be confused and completely traumatized. Everything that she had ever known and loved was gone. And she would never know why. *Poor Winnie*. Caroline was feeling badly for Winnie even before they had met.

Chapter 12: At Last

At last, it was their turn. The volunteer checked their paperwork and reached up to a cage on the top row. Unlocking the cage, she lifted a very chubby puppy out of her cage. A bouncing bundle of fluff, floppy ears, and furry paws was lowered slowly and placed in Caroline's open arms. Winnie was here! And what a surprise! Winnie looked exactly like Snugs! Exactly, except for a few extra pounds! She was quite a chubby little lady.

It was love at first sight. Whimpering with joy, Winnie proceeded to give Caroline and Tom thorough face washes. It was as if this curly bundle of joy had known them for years. As Tom drove home, laughing and relieved, Winnie enthusiastically continued to plaster wet kisses all over Caroline's face. So much love. Nobody seemed to mind the pouring rain. Or even notice it.

Winnie seemed to adore her new foster mom and dad. And the feeling was mutual. Even after a few minutes of hugging this chunky little lady, Caroline knew that it was going to be hard to let her go. Winnie was irresistible. The new family, whoever that might eventually be, would be adopting the perfect family pet. Looking at her beautiful face, Caroline vowed to foster Winnie as long as needed to allow Nancy enough time to find the best home for her. Winnie, this lost little lady, deserved the most loving home possible. She deserved some happiness after all she had been through, and would be welcome to stay in the Quinn home for as long as needed. Until Nancy found a perfect forever family, this darling spaniel would be safe and well cared for in her foster home.

Chapter 13: Home, Sweet Home

When they arrived at the Quinn's home, Winnie raced into house, checking out each room and even running out to the backyard to have a quick peek. Wagging her tail faster than one could ever imagine possible, it seemed that her stubby little tail might fly right off! What a bundle of energy! As she gleefully wiggled and jiggled her chubby little hips, she won Caroline and Tom over immediately and completely. Winnie was a winner!

Tom joked that Winnie was an appropriate name for the plump little lady, since she was the same shape as a Winnebago. Caroline, though, didn't like the old-fashioned name. It didn't seem to suit her playful personality. So, after some discussion, Winnie was re-named Jazzy Joy. Now Caroline and Jazzy shared the same middle name. Like her name, she was a bouncy gal and as charming as could be.

After devouring her first meal in a split second, the full-figured beauty went for her first walk around the block in the rain. Due to her extra weight, she seemed to be out of breath at times and was clearly out of shape. Caroline guessed that she had not had regular exercise for quite a while, and wondered if her previous owners had been sick or too elderly to take Winnie for daily walks. Everything would be sorted out in time. For now, Jazzy was home and she had brought a new sense of wonder and joy to her newfound family, just when they needed it most.

That night, the pleasingly plump, very curly spaniel walked into the Quinn home and straight into Caroline and Tom's hearts. Safe and warm, with the rain beating down outside, Jazzy Joy cooed softly, snuggling between her delighted new owners. All was well. Jazzy was home … her forever home. There was no way Jazzy Joy was going to be adopted by anyone else. The Quinn home was now Jazzy Joy's forever home. Fostering Jazzy went out the window and Caroline couldn't wait to call Nancy in the morning.

When Caroline called Nancy, telling her that they wanted to start the adoption process, Nancy was thrilled to hear the news, but not too surprised. What a difference a day makes. A couple of weeks ago, everything had been set in motion for the Quinns to become a foster family. But it seemed that God had other plans. In just a few minutes, Jazzy had turned that plan upside down. The adoption papers would be signed as soon as possible.

Chapter 14: Christmas Day

Six days later, on Christmas morning, the colorful lights twinkled on the tree. The spaniel ornaments were stunning, and Jazzy Joy's stocking was filled to the brim with treats. In just six days, Jazzy had begun to magically transform the Quinn home. As Caroline attended to Jazzy's every need, it was like having a child again, and she loved being needed. But everything was not perfect.

There was disappointment woven into the day too. David had not been able to come home for the holidays due to his military duties. He was dearly missed. They family planned to chat with and see David via Skype. Introducing Jazzy to David was going to be the highlight in the day.

Although there is no way the new dog could ever replace a missing son, Jazzy, in her own way, was already starting to fill in some of the gaps in the most amazing ways. She was always right by Caroline's side. It was so comforting to feel the warmth of Jazzy Joy as she snuggled up as close as possible to her new mom. Jazzy seemed to know that all was not well. Caroline was worried about David, knowing that life in the military was very challenging, stressful, and dangerous at times. It was upsetting to know that Christmas in the military was just another day of working as usual. There would not be a Christmas dinner prepared for the troops while they were far from their families in Germany. How she wished she could send him a delicious turkey dinner with all the fixings. This was not the way it should be.

Every morning for many years, Tom and Caroline had prayed that God would bless and protect their beloved sons. When the boys were little, Tom and Caroline could keep them safe. But now, David and Daniel were on their own, and all they could do was to continue to pray for God's best in their lives. As parents of adult children, it was hard to let go.

On a brighter note, Caroline's heart was full as she watched Dan bustling around the tree, choosing gifts and being a jolly good Santa. What a blessing it was to watch her husband and Dan, their dear son, opening their gifts. Caressing Jazzy's silky, velvety ears, Caroline smiled and thought of Snuggles. She knew that Snugs would be so pleased to know that Jazzy Joy had arrived just in time for Christmas. Snugs and Jazzy had so much in common. What stood out the most was that both dogs had come into their lives in time for Christmas. Whispering a prayer of thanks, Caroline was at peace.

When Gramma Quinn, Tom's mom, arrived for Christmas dinner, Jazzy showered her with tons of kisses. Giggling and laughing, Gramma tried to dodge being plastered with more kisses. But Jazzy won that tussle. Jazzy totally believed that one could never have too many kisses. They become instant friends. Everything seemed better when there was a happy dog wagging her tail wildly, no matter what. In the years to come, Jazzy visited Gramma Quinn many times at her home, treating all of the residents to lots of kisses. One lady even asked for a photo of Jazzy. She had everyone laughing their heads off when she announced that she wanted her boyfriend to be as affectionate as Jazzy. It was too funny.

The best part of the day was having the family chat with David. Technology was such a gift when loved ones were so far away. David met Jazzy Joy for the first time via Skype, and, as expected, David was thrilled to meet her and to know that his mom was so happy. David also commented on her chubby little body and highly recommended getting Jazzy on a strict diet and exercise routine immediately. He was right. Caroline promised that tomorrow they would all turn over a new leaf. Less food and more exercise. Absolutely. In the meantime, Caroline decided it would be best not to tell David that Jazzy had just feasted on turkey, potatoes, and pumpkin pie, just like Snugs had done for so many years.

Like Snuggles, Jazzy loved to eat. From day one, it was crystal clear that food was her love language. She always seemed to be looking for her next meal. Perhaps her food obsession was because she remembered being hungry when she was homeless and was afraid it might happen again. Tom joked that judging by the look of her, he was quite sure that she had not been homeless for very long. And he was quite sure that she had not missed many meals. Convinced that she had not suffered too much, he teased Caroline by saying that she had likely spent most of her time on the streets somewhere between the bakery and the butcher. Ouch!! Oh well … the diet would start tomorrow. For sure.

Chapter 15: New Beginnings

Jazzy's rescue story was just the beginning. We rescued Jazzy five years ago, and she continues to rescue us every day. Hiking is so much fun again. Jazzy is a trail blazer! My piano students absolutely adore Jazzy, and she greets them eagerly each week. Kisses and face washes from Jazzy are part of our daily routine, and we start the day with a wet black nose pressing into our faces as Jazzy brings us socks. After making her selection for the sock of the day, she presents them with great enthusiasm every morning. We believe she thinks that socks are like roses. Not quite, Jazzy.

When Jazzy first arrived, her extra weight was affecting her breathing. She was often panting and short of breath. Thankfully, with lots of walks, hiking, and healthy foods, Jazzy quickly dropped almost ten pounds. Both Jazzy and I launched into the Paleo Diet. Eating lots of plain chicken, apples, carrots, and no carbs, the once-chunky little butterball is now quite the stunning little lady. She is now in great shape. We both are! Teamwork works every time.

Running up and down the trails with her ears flapping away continues to be quite a sight to see. Tom pointed out that she does twice the elevation that we do. Racing down to check on me, who is usually a little slower, especially on the steeper parts, Jazzy then zooms back up the trail to check on Tom. After checking on her pack, she bounds ahead for a few minutes, checking out all the interesting smells, and then heads down again to check on me. We are so grateful that, with all of her exploring and investigating, so far, she has not run into a skunk or raccoon. Or a bear. Yikes! We are keeping our fingers crossed for uneventful hikes in the future.

My boys, Daniel and David, tease me by insisting that Jazzy is my favorite child. They often point out that the biggest photos in our home are of Jazzy. Tom also teases me when I make something special for Jazzy to eat. He makes me laugh when he asks if he could possibly have any of the leftovers. I always assure him that there is more than enough for both he and Jazzy and that he will always be my first love.

Jazzy has traveled thousands of miles with us across America and Canada, and she has brought laughter and joy to all that she meets. My parents were delighted with Jazzy when we visited them often while on sabbatical in Canada. Her unconditional love has sustained us through some tough times. If you have a dog, or have ever had a dog, you will know what I am talking about. On harder days, she just seems to understand. Her comforting eyes seem to say everything that is needed. Her reassuring paw on my arm seems to be her way of reminding me that everything will be alright. I love it when she rests her head on my arm, wanting some attention. She is my best girl. I have a sign that says it best. *My therapist has a black wet nose.*

She is our gift. If we all were as kind to others as our dogs are to us, what a wonderful world it would be. I tell Jazzy that I need to go to church to become a better person, but she doesn't need to attend since she is already perfect.

Jazzy is always ready to sneak in a kiss or two or three. In my opinion, she gives so much love. In Tom's opinion, Jazzy gives so much slobber. Ouch again! Throughout each day, Jazzy, my furry guardian angel, is always by my side. Sometimes we chat through the day and I tell her what's going on and she replies with appropriate grunts and sighs, and seems to understand so much. Jazzy likes to be fed on time, and if I am late or forget I will soon feel her paw on my leg with her worried, concerned eyes gazing up at me. At this point, I drop everything and take care of Jazzy. At night, we fall asleep to her musical coos and contented sighs.

And snoring. Although it might be hard to believe, our little princess snores almost as loudly as Tom. Tom says that she snores even louder. All is well. She is our miracle! Our miracle dog, Jazzy Joy!

A Message to my Readers

Dear Readers,

I have had fun writing this story and hope you enjoyed it, too. Although it is a Christmas story, it is a story that can be shared with others at any time of the year. Sometimes, we need a little Christmas to brighten our spirits. It is important for you to know that, while I was writing this story, our country was struggling in the COVID-19 pandemic. The Coronavirus had caused a worldwide pandemic. Businesses, churches, restaurants, schools, universities, and so much more were closed. Families were isolated from their loved ones. It was a time of great uncertainty, with many wondering if we would ever return to our normal lives. For many, it was a time of great loss. Due to the need for isolation, families were banned from visiting loved ones in hospitals, and their loved ones passed on alone and isolated, with no one to hold their hand. Our own family faced deep loss. My mom lost her battle with pancreatic cancer, and I was not allowed to go and see her due to the pandemic restrictions. It was heartbreaking. Tragically, there was also great unrest in our country, and we continue to pray for much-needed healing.

The good news is that there is still so much goodness to be experienced and shared. More than ever, we must look for the good. We all must keep shining brightly and wait together for easier times. They will come. We must keep hope alive. As we wait together, I want to encourage you to look for your own miracles. Miracles, large and small, do happen. I wish you every joy and blessing in all you do.

I saved one of the best parts until the end. Enjoy the photos of Snuggles and Jazzy.

You can reach me at cjoyquinn@gmail.com. I would love to hear from you. Please feel free to contact me and let me know that you enjoyed the story.

Caroline Joy Quinn
October 2021

Photos of Snugs and Jazzy

Snuggles, our prince of the planet. I know he would have loved Jazzy.

A fun hike at Barclay Lake, WA.

Do you like Jazzy's penguin sweater? David didn't, and every time he came over, he took it off Jazz and hid it.

A snowy walk in a blustery cold day hiking along the Skykomish River in the Cascades. Hmmmm….it's time for Jazzy to get a haircut.

This is Jazzy's New Year's Eve dress. David didn't like this one either. Giggles.

Jazzy checking her email while I teach nearby. Smiles.

Jazzy sneaking in a quick kiss instead of looking at the camera. So much love!

Christmas family photo in 2019. Both boys were home.   And Jazzy, as always, was front and center stealing the show.

Jazzy...well prepared with a sock and her favorite stuffie.

At the top of Oyster Dome near Bellingham, WA. After a hard climb, the views were just spectacular. Jazzy loves to run up and down the trails checking on me and then races back to catch up with Tom. She loves to be the leader of her pack.

Happy times at Mount Hood, Oregon.

Jazzy Joy, our little princess.

Jazzy loves all the piano students.

Christmas morning Dec 2019.

There is always time for a quick kiss.

Taking a nap after working hard being adorable.

Covid times prevented entertaining in our home, so we had picnics instead. We had great fun catching up with Tom's students at beautiful parks. Jazzy made everything even better.

Are you interested in fostering a dog?

https://www.rover.com/blog/dog-fostering-101/

The above link is a great resource to get you started.

There are so many dogs in shelters that need a new home.

Jazzy Joy was a a foster dog, and we fell in love with her immediately. Perhaps the same will happen to you.

If you can, please consider fostering a dog while they wait for their forever home. Sometimes the dogs just need some training as they learn to trust others and be the best they can be.

Talk to your local pet shelter and learn more. They will be able to help you through the process. You can make a difference by saving lives.

Fostering a dog, or adopting a rescue dog may or may not be for you, but it is a wonderful option for the right family.

About the Author

Caroline Joy Quinn lives in Seattle, Washington with her husband. Together they enjoy hiking and traveling. Being a piano teacher has brought her much joy for many years. She enjoys cooking for her boys, walking with friends, reading, playing her piano and puttering in the garden. Caroline's newest adventure is being a Real Estate Broker. She is also a international best selling author in the Power of Why anthology dedicated to encouraging other musicians in their journeys.

Caroline hopes this book will bless and encourage readers everywhere to look for their own miracles as their life stories unfold. Her faith in God is a central part of her life and her greatest source of strength over the years. She believes that every good gift comes from God. Jazzy Joy was such a gift.